Dancing Dragon Magic

Insight Journal

Susan Smith James

DANCING DRAGON MAGIC: INSIGHT JOURNAL

Published by Happy Publishing,
www.HappyPublishing.net

www.DancingDragonMagic.com

Playing with the Dragons!

When I first started writing
Dancing Dragon Magic: Dialogues in Clay,
tuning into the dragon energy felt unusual.
Having worked with this energy for several
years now, I have come to appreciate the
nuances of the various dragons and the vast
variety of energies they command. This
book is a way for everyone to connect with
the dragons, in all their subtleties and
strengths. This journal is really a journey
into the Dragon Realm.
Spread your intuitive wings and glide on
the energetic fields that the dragons play
in. This journey is meant to be fun and the
dragons promise to be gentle!

"I hope you enjoy your travels here!"
Susan Smith James

1 The Sun Dragon

"Greetings, I am The Sun Dragon. I bring light into the world. Darkness flees from me. My heat burns away all that does not serve you. Do not come close to me unless you are prepared to give up the past and be forever changed!"

What needs illuminating?

2 The Night Dragon

"Breathe in the stillness of the night. I am with you when troubles plague you in your sleep. Fear has no place to rest, where I am. I will give you courage, even in the darkest night."

What do you fear?

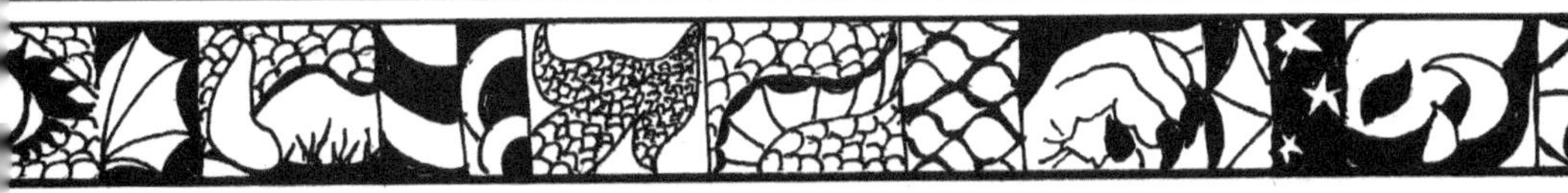

3 The Cloud Dragon

"Let the gentle breeze move you. Feel the warmth of the day lift you up. Light and shadow both play with me. I bring soft, loving, joy to all who seek me. I will hold you in my arms, like a mother holds her child!"

How can my love serve you?

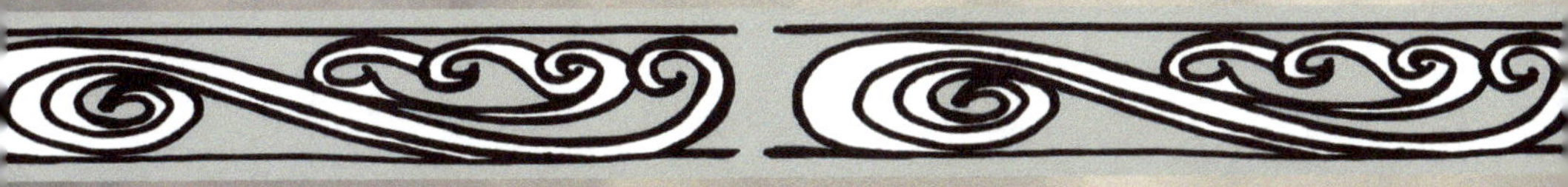

4 The Day Dragon

"Rainbows form wherever I go. Dancing and singing come forth magically, in my presence. Seek me out to lift your spirits, to amplify your joy of life. There can be nothing but happy laughter, when I am with you."

What joy may I bring you?

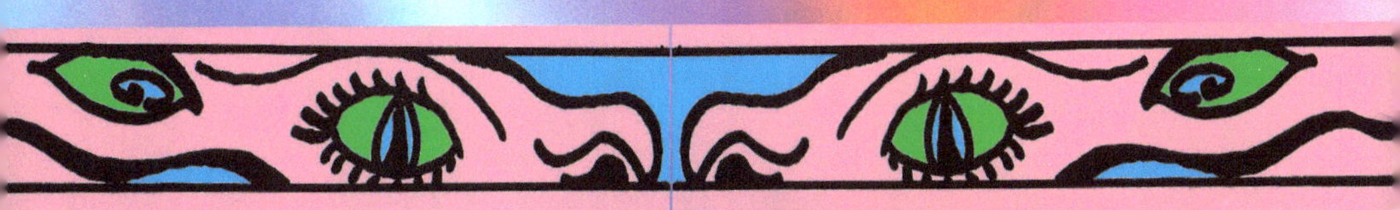

5 The Sea Dragon

"Feel my size and my power. I can move great obstacles from your life. Nothing is too much for me to push away. Seek me out if you need assistance. You may ride on my back, over any troubled seas.

Where do you wish to travel?

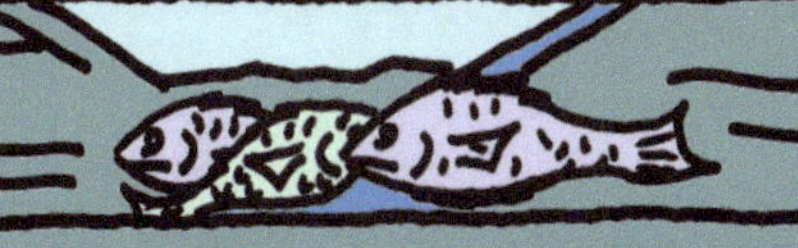
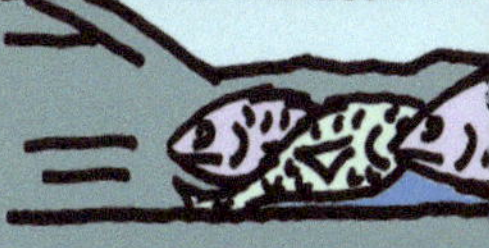

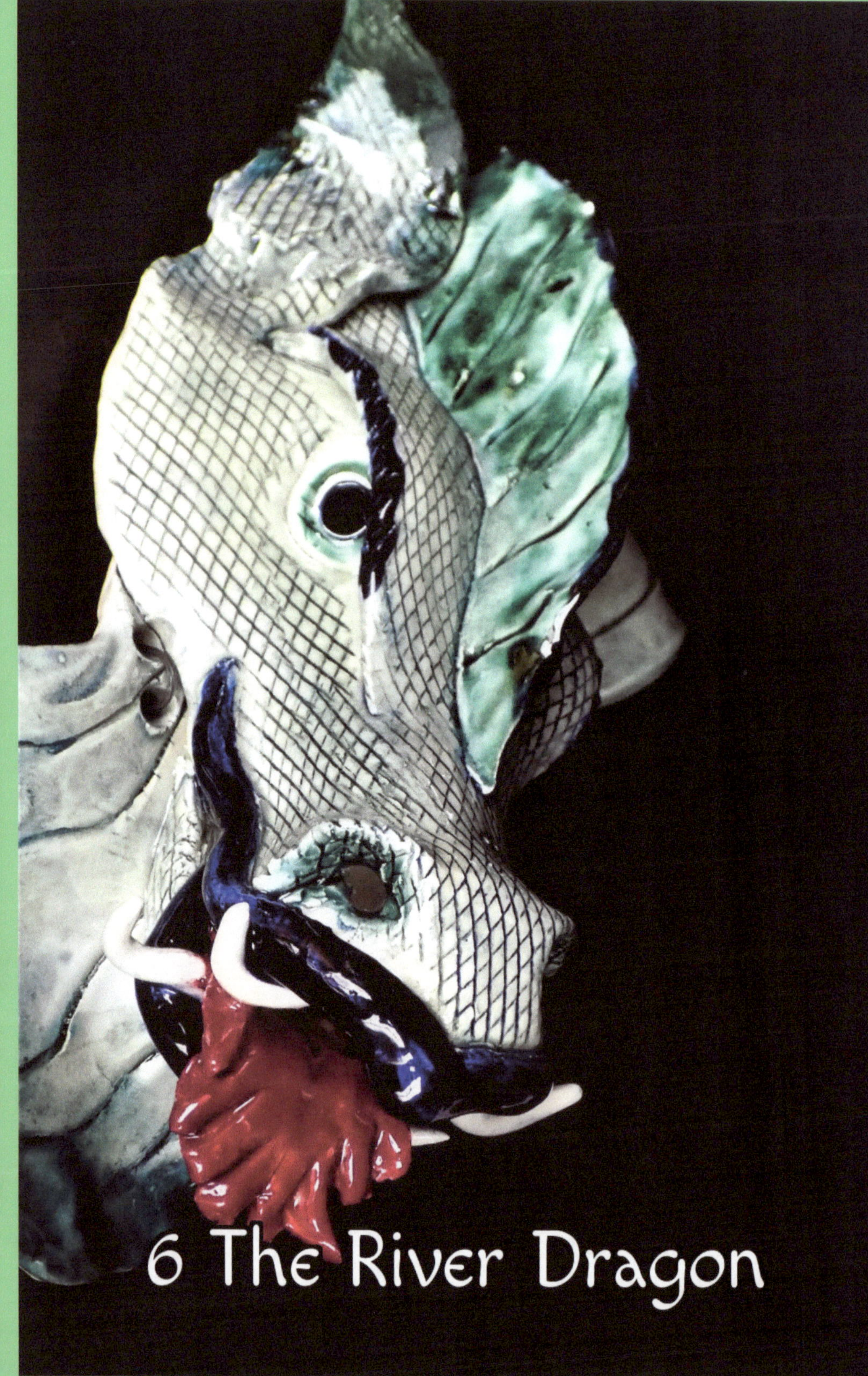

6 The River Dragon

"I bring flow into your life. Creativity comes with me. If you feel small, I can make you bigger. If you seek quiet and meditation, I can assist you. I am a babbling brook, I am a mighty waterfall, I am The River Dragon!"

How may I serve you?

7 The Smoke Dragon

"What is that smell? I am the remnants of your past experiences, only a dark smudge that is left in your memory. Take heart, for the smoke will dissipate, the air will clear. I will purify your soul and carry your past troubles away!"

What do you need to clear away?

8 The Rain Dragon

*"Some will find me to be trouble, but I am
necessary to cleanse your world. Enjoy
the washing that I bring. Inhale the smell
of clean fresh air, after I have passed.
I never linger long."*

What should be washed away?

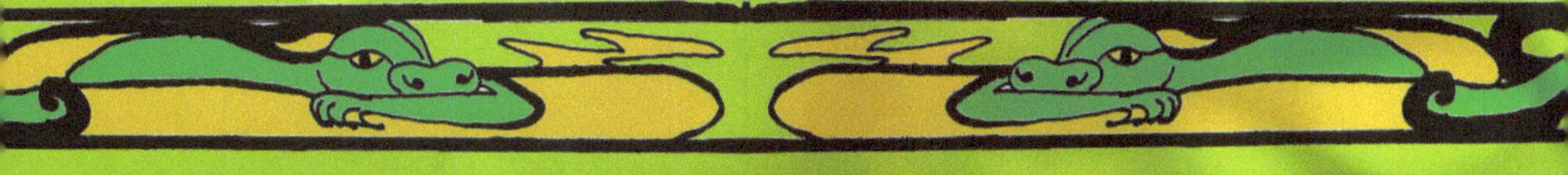

9 The Ocean Dragon

"I live at the bottom of the ocean. I am clever and cunning. I will construct great devices for you. I give your ideas a deep footing in the world. Creativity and wealth well up through me. I am ready to assist you in any business plans."

What are your goals, dreams and desires?

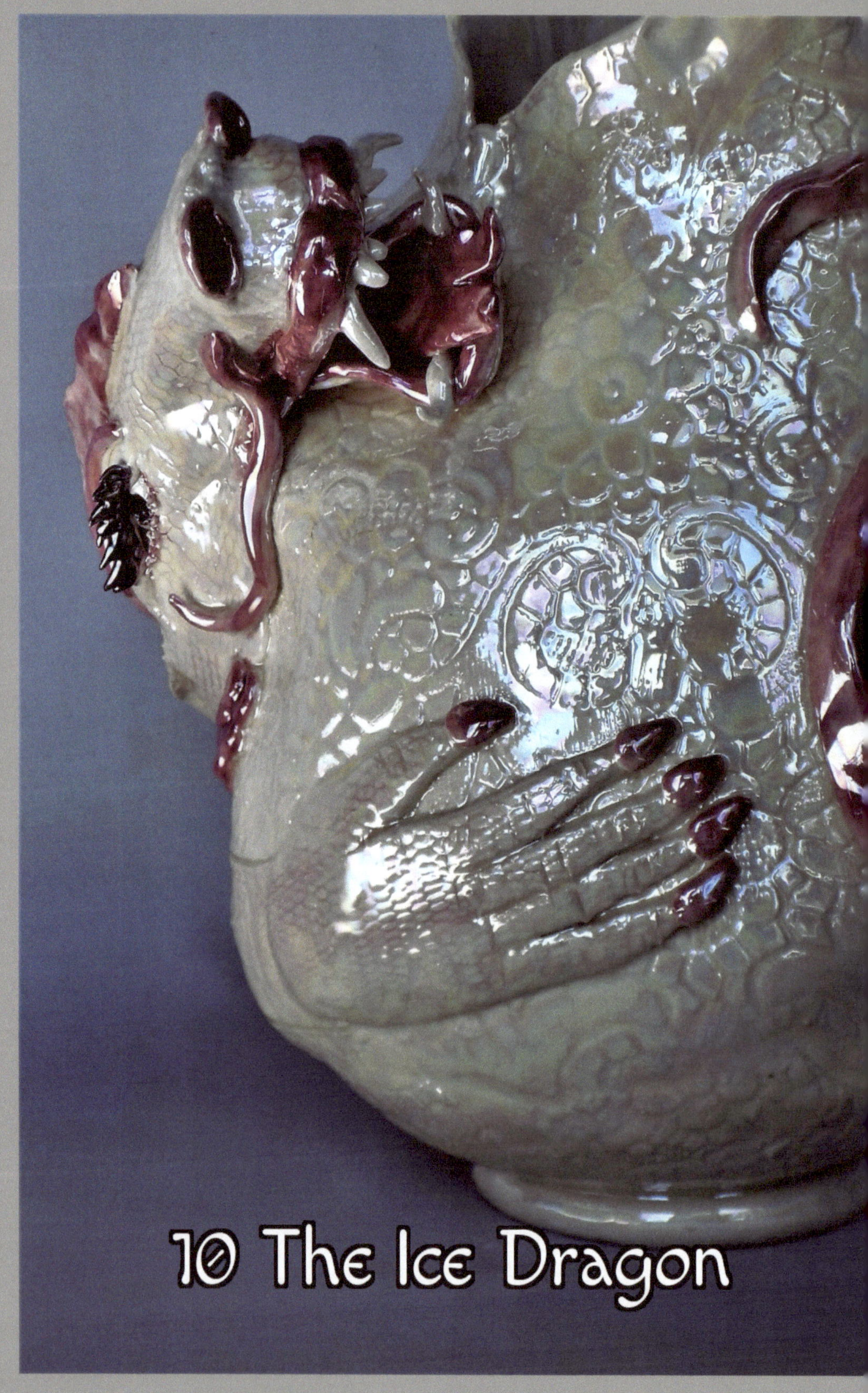

10 The Ice Dragon

"Like the prism of a crystal, I see all sides of a problem at once. Distilling it down to a single point, out of which perfect decisions can be made. Seek me out when you need clear vision. Ask for my advice."

What do you wish me to know?

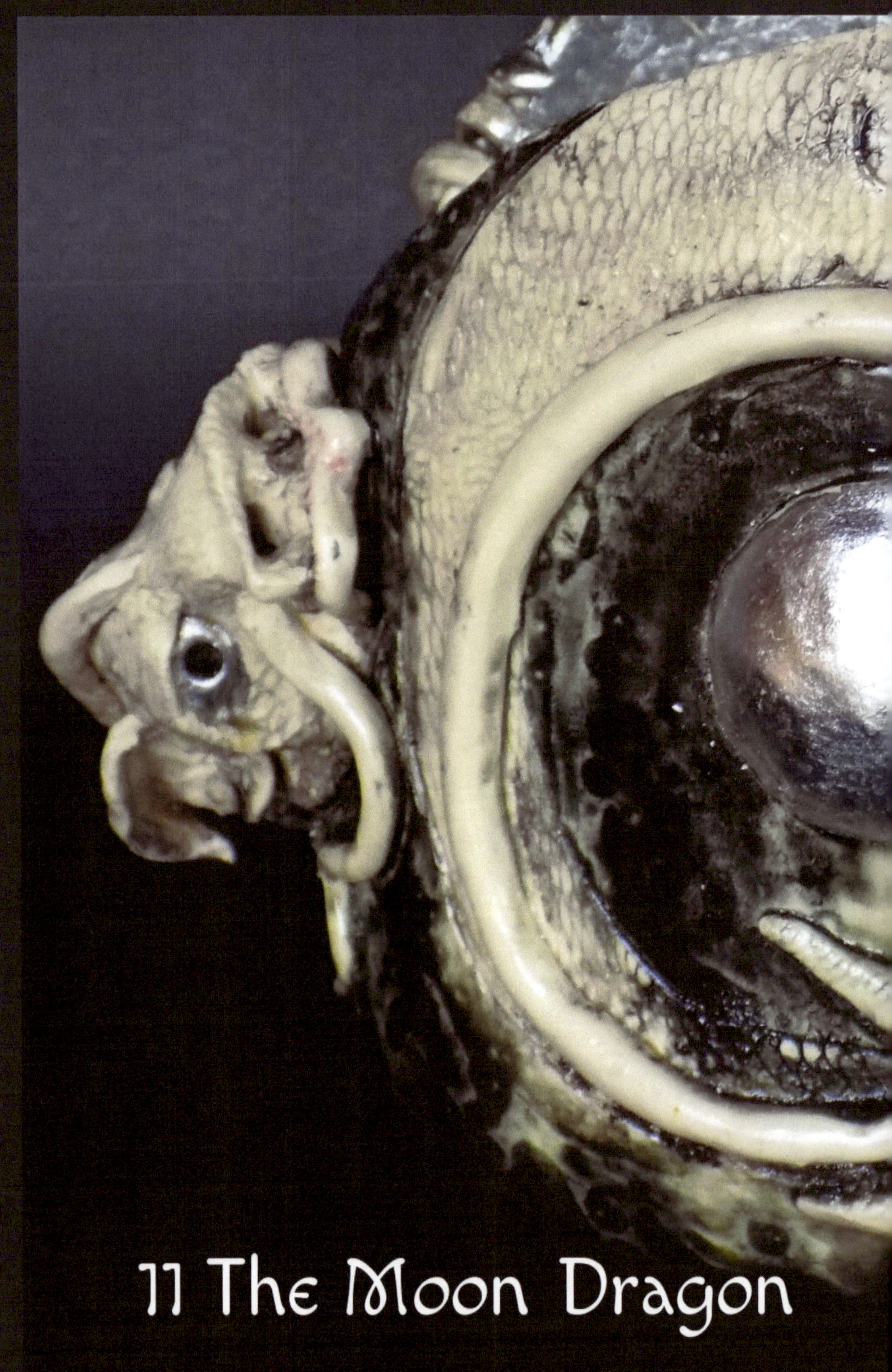

11 The Moon Dragon

"Peace is my mission. Allow me to bring calm and tranquility into your life. Seek me when the chaos of the world becomes too much. Sit with me and I will show you the way of Peace."

Where do you look for peace in your life?

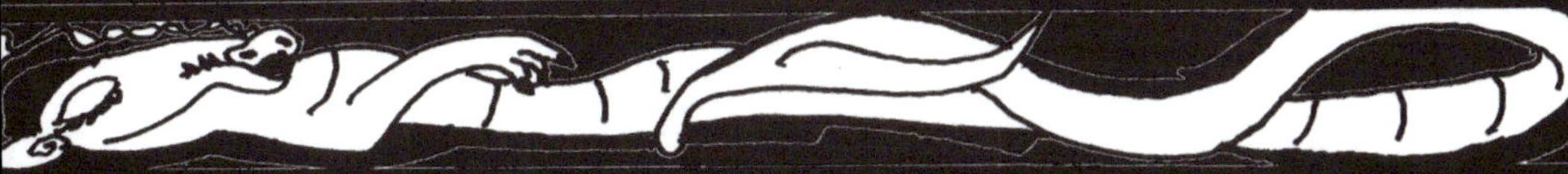

12 Icthianna, The Merdragon

"I am 'Peace Incarnate' there can be no struggle in my presence. Harmony and love come with me. There is no place hidden from me, nowhere I cannot go. Rejoice at my arrival for peace will stay with you when I leave."

What hidden turmoil do you have?

13 The Vine Dragon

What do you desire to feed?

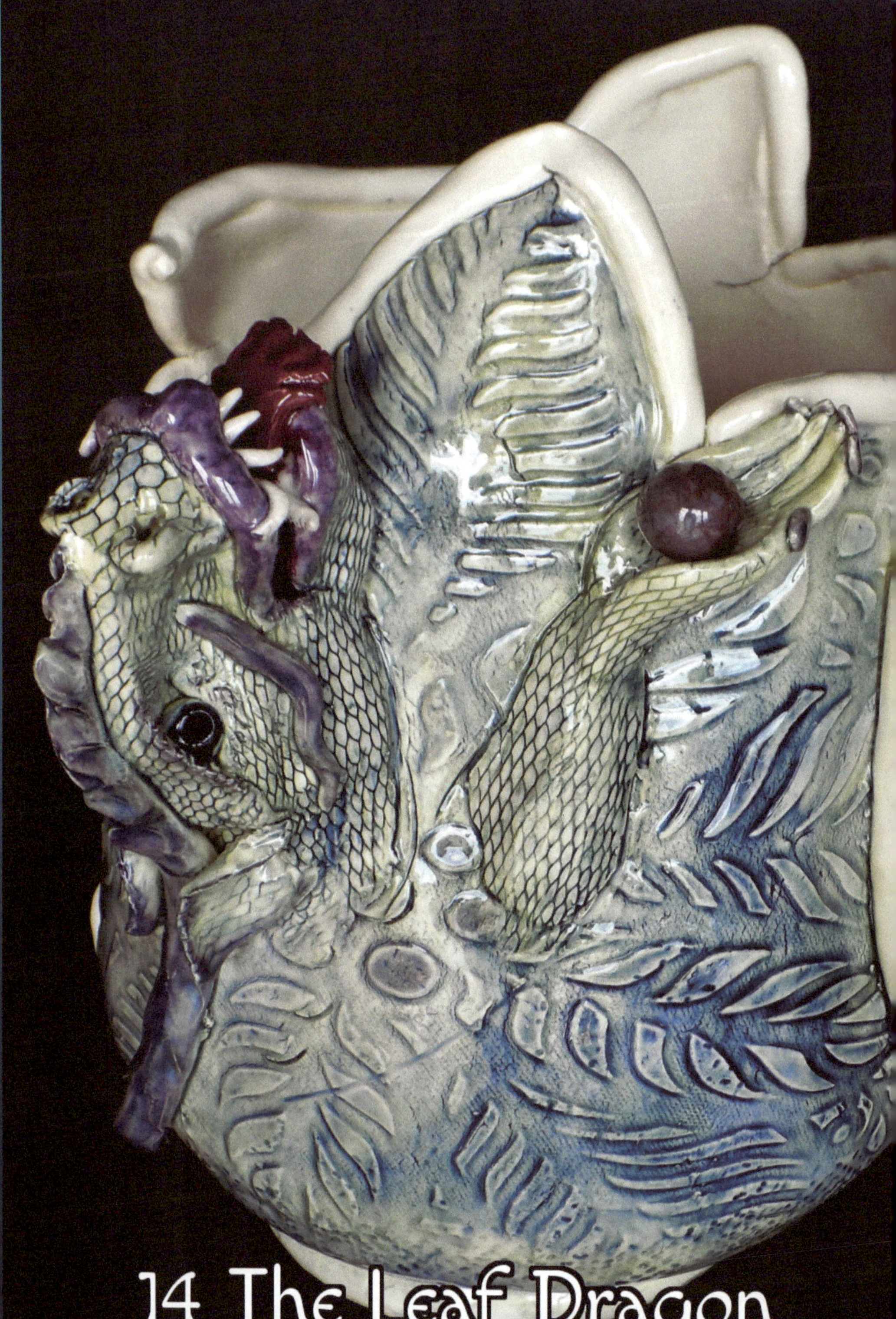

14 The Leaf Dragon

"I am hidden in the deep forest, I am difficult to find, but watch your step or you may tread on me. I will help you with long concealed things, together we can find the camouflaged parts of your soul, and mend the bruised and broken substance of your being."

What have you concealed?

15 Dragon Fire

What needs to be burned away? What old items should you melt into something new?

How can dragon fire assist in transforming your life?

16 Dragon Strength

Our strength is immense. What can be lifted for you?
What can be moved for your higher good?

17 Dragon Flight

Where do you need to go? Hop on your dragon and ask to be taken there. Be prepared to fly very high!

18 Dragon Magic

We have powerful magic. What transformation do you require? Be careful how you use this magic, what you have transformed, you can never change back!

19 Dragon Love

Our capacity for love is great. Feel the power of it, let the dragon's love fill your entire being. Allow yourself to be moved by the power of dragon love!
How can Dragon Love serve you?

20 Dragon Dance

Dragons love to dance! We dance in joy, exuberance and pleasure. To dance with a dragon is to become one with the universe, to be one with God!

Share how you can dance with the dragons!

21 Dragon Hunt

We will help you find your goal. Ask
and we will show the way.
What is it that you hunt?

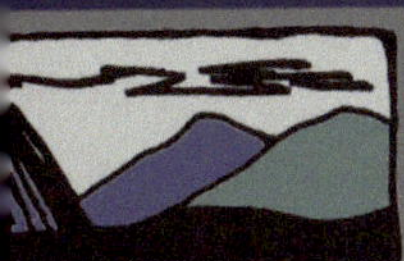

22 Dragon Teeth

Sharp and powerful, our teeth can destroy and consume. What do you wish to uncreate in your life? Be careful, for what a dragon destroys cannot be brought back!

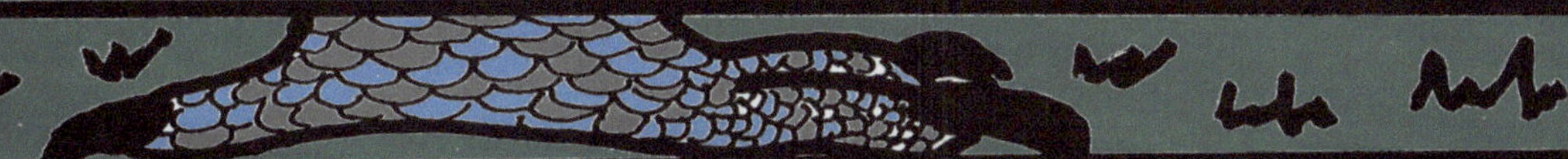

23 Dragon Wisdom

We have existed for eons, with our long lives comes great wisdom. How may we assist you in your search for knowledge? We are happy to impart as much wisdom as you are ready to receive.

24 Dragon Rest

Lay your head down at our feet, close your eyes and rest. We will guard you, assuage your fears and give you a chance to rest without worry. Hush now, and be still. What should to be put to rest?

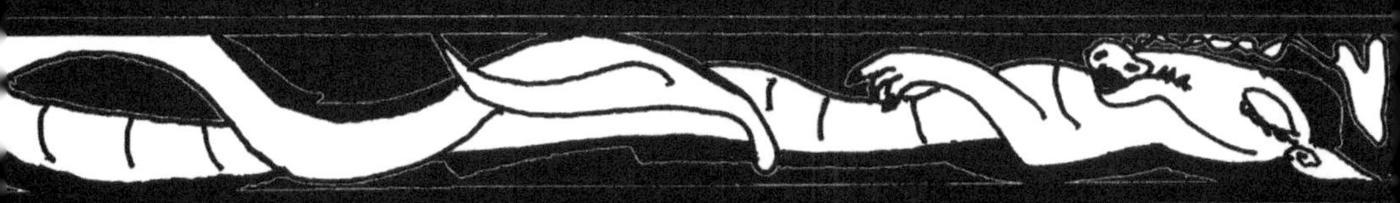

25 Dragon Hand

My hand is strong and has sharp claws.
How can I assist you in your quest?
Do you wish something opened, or
something crushed?

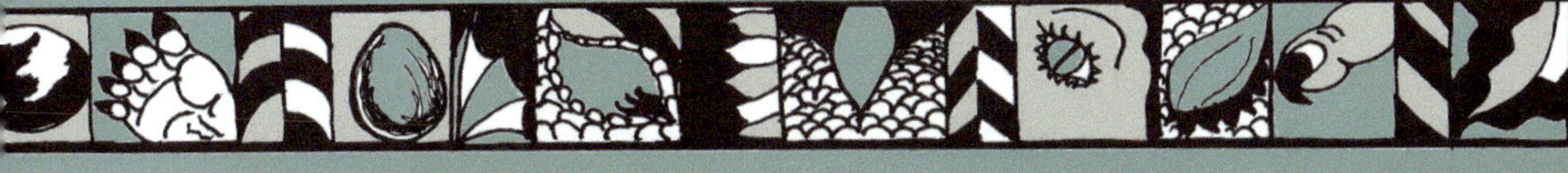

26 Dragon Tail

A dragon's tail is full of magic, but is not
easily controlled. It tends to whip
around, as if it has a mind of its own,
but point it in the right direction,
and it can create miracles!
What miracles do you intend?

27 Dragon Sight

A dragon does not see as a human does.
Look through our eyes and see the
world differently. You will see farther
and deeper with dragon sight.
What do you wish to see in a new way?

28 Dragon Tongue

We can sense more than just taste with our tongues. Our tongues can pick up heat, movement, energy and breath.
How can this sense help you?

29 Dragon Gift

We hold out a special gift, just for you.
It will appear in your moment of need.
Always Expect it!
When will that moment be?

30 Dragon Swim

Water dragons swim as well as air dragons
fly. We will carry you through any water.
Where are you destined to go?

31 Dragon Debate

When dragons get together, there is
always much to say.
Do you need us to speak on your behalf,
do you wish to discuss an idea?
We are happy to assist.

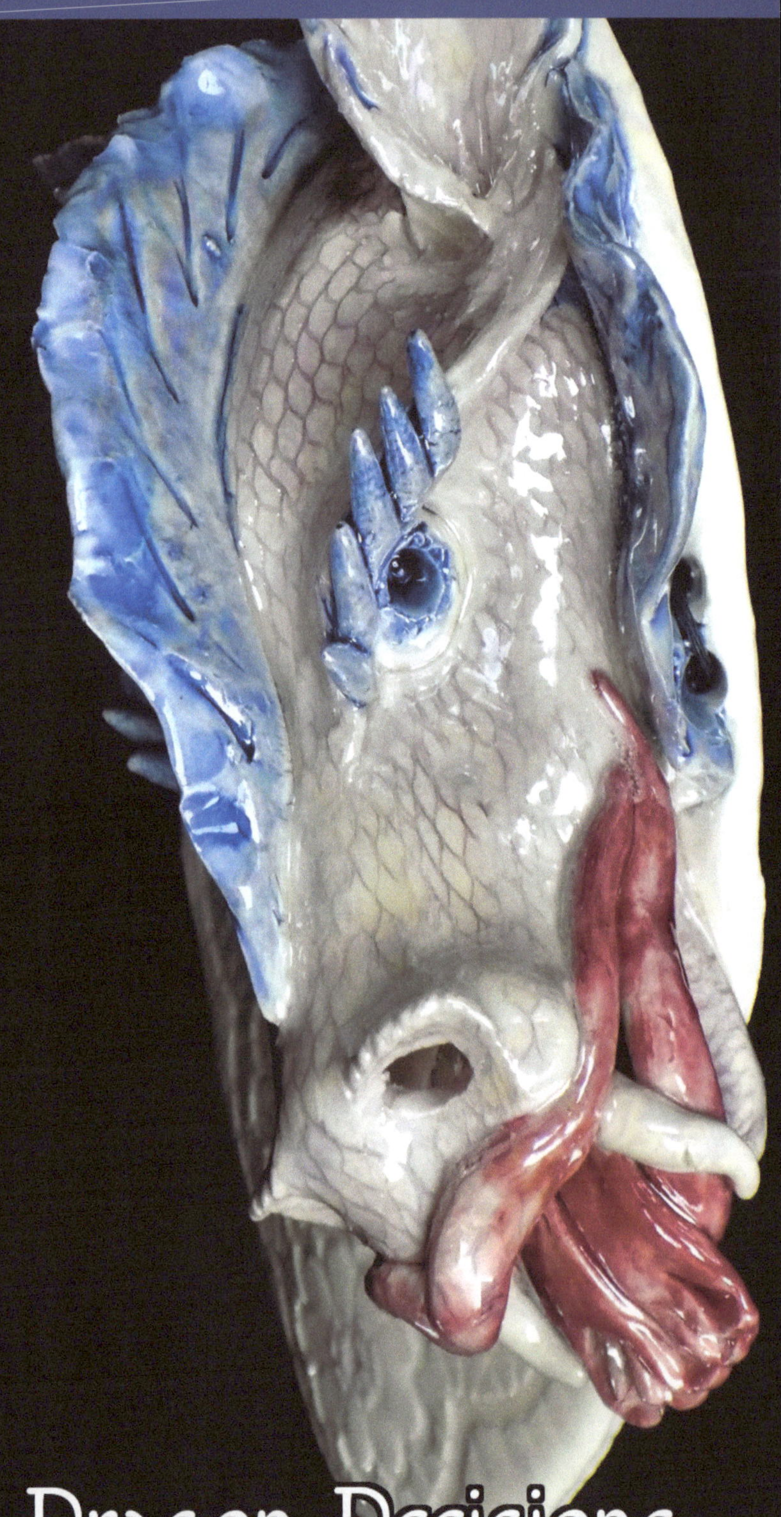

32 Dragon Decisions

We are decisive creatures; seldom do we take long to decide. We will not fail to come to the best choice. Let us assist you! What is your dilemma?

33 Dragon Song

Dragons love to sing. Listen closely and we will form a song just for you. Can you hear it? Can you feel it's resonance in your heart? Write your song!

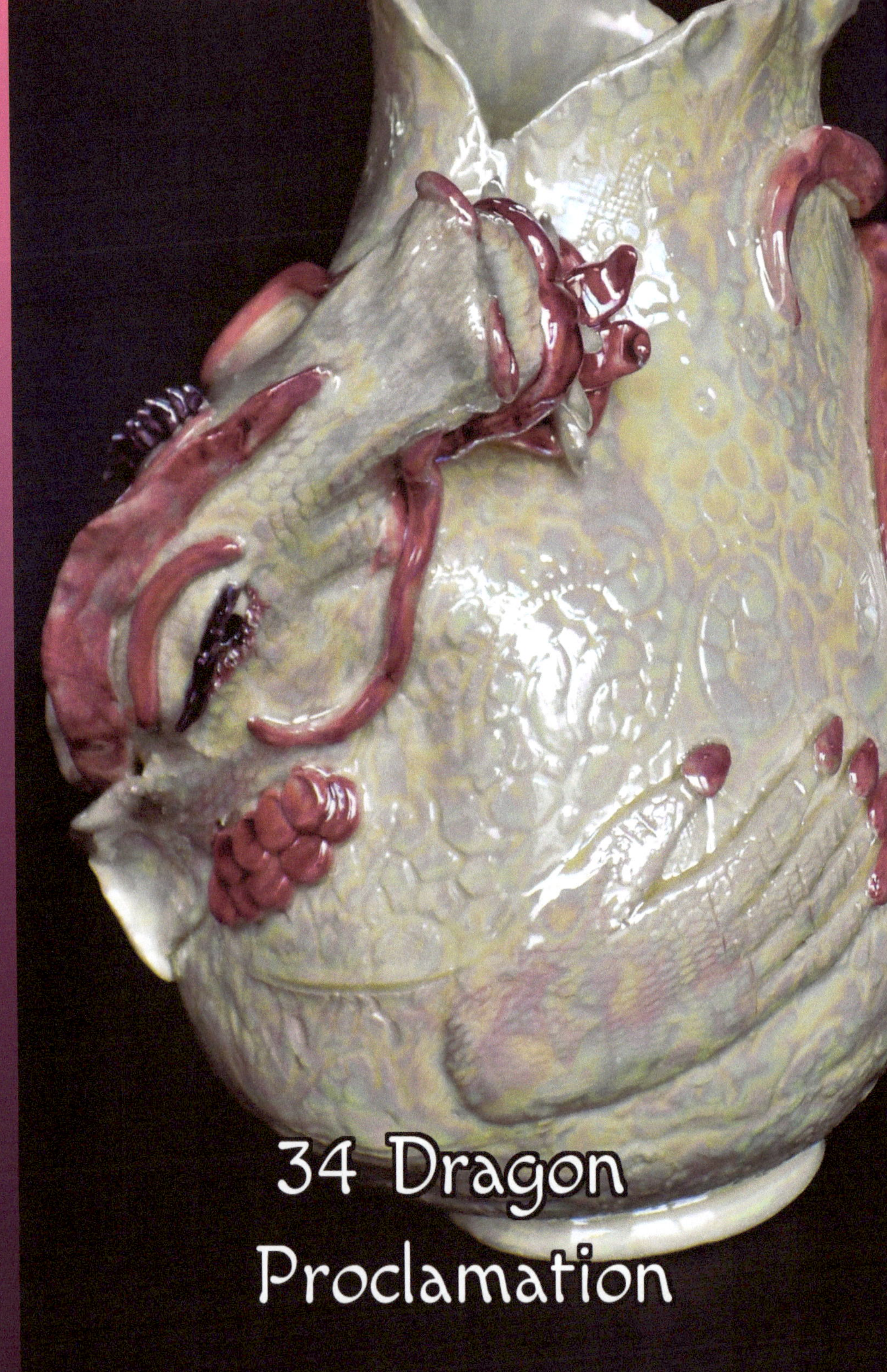

34 Dragon
Proclamation

What needs to be declared in your life? We will proclaim it from the highest mountain for you. Everyone will see, hear, feel your proclamation!

VATICINIA,
Siue
PROPHETIÆ
Abbatis
IOACHIMI
&
Anselmi Episcopi

Cum imaginibus ære incisis correctione et pulcritudine, plurium manuscriptorum exemplariu ope, et uariaru imagin tabulis, et delineationibu aliis impressis longe præstantiora.

QVIBVS RO
Oraculum Turcicum siderationis
maxim
adiecta sunt.
m Prefatione,
et Adnotation
Paschalini
Regiselmi

VATICINII,
ouero
PROFETIE
dell Abb
GIOACHINO,
e di
Anselmo Vescouo
di Marsico,

Con l'imagin
ate in rame, di corre
aggiore, che gl'altri sin
giuto di molti exempla
ri scritti à penna et uer
le piture, et aisegni di ua
rie imagini.

una Ruota, et un'Oraco
lo Turchesco di
ma cosideratione.
Insieme con la Prefatione,
et Annotat
Pasqualino
Regiselmo.

35 Dragon Heart

A dragon's heart holds the power of creation.
What do you need to create in your life?
How can a dragon's heart serve you?

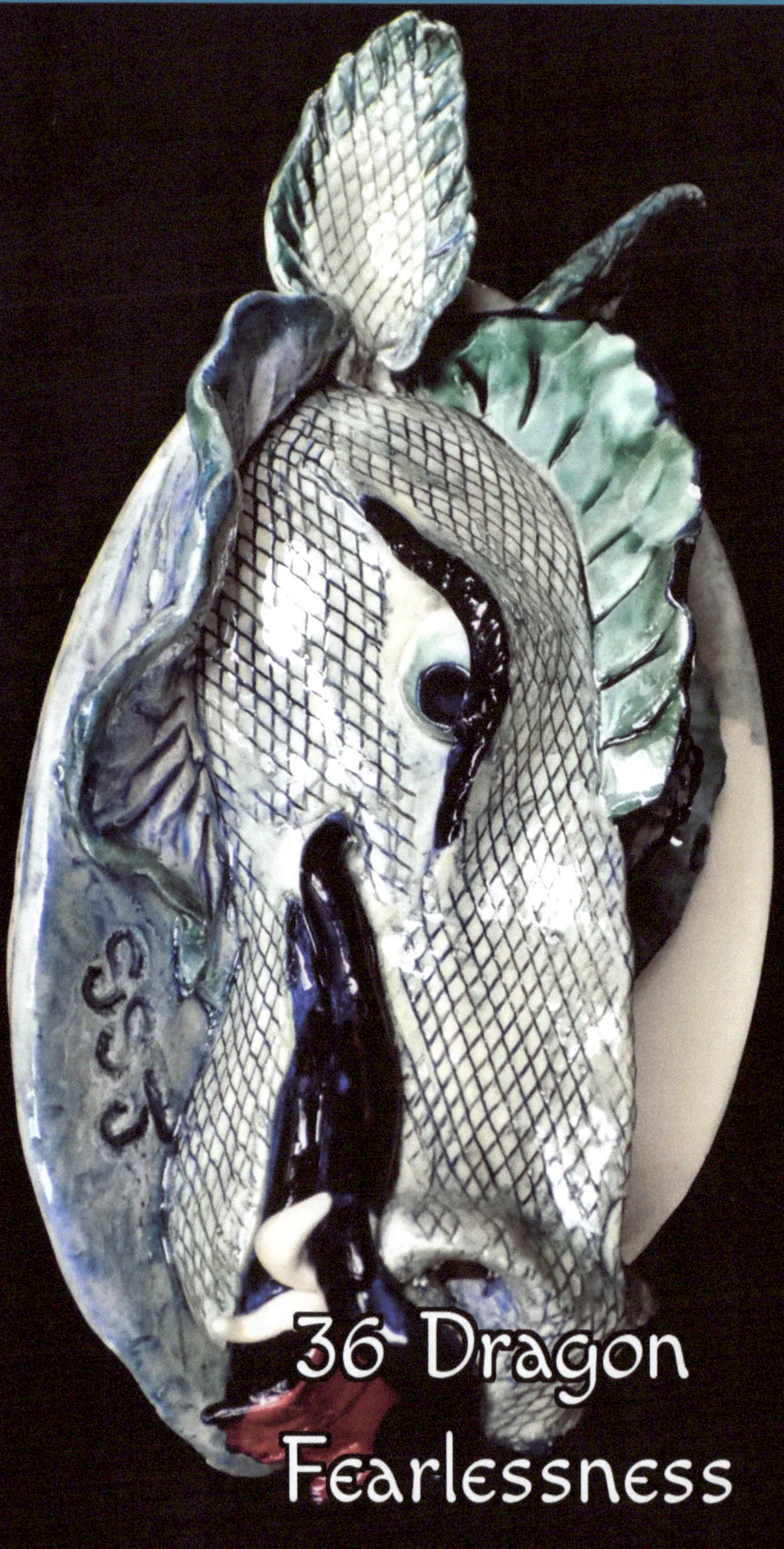

36 Dragon
Fearlessness

The first rule of being a dragon is:
DO NOT BE AFRAID.
How can a dragon's fearlessness serve you?
What are you afraid of?

37 Dragon Counsel

What is your trouble? What do you need
help with? We will give you counsel
and find answers to your problems.
Rest safely in our guidance.

38 Dragon Hatchlings

Our young are cherished beyond measure.
Feel the joy, love, hope, and promise
that a newly hatched dragon evokes.
What do you feel?

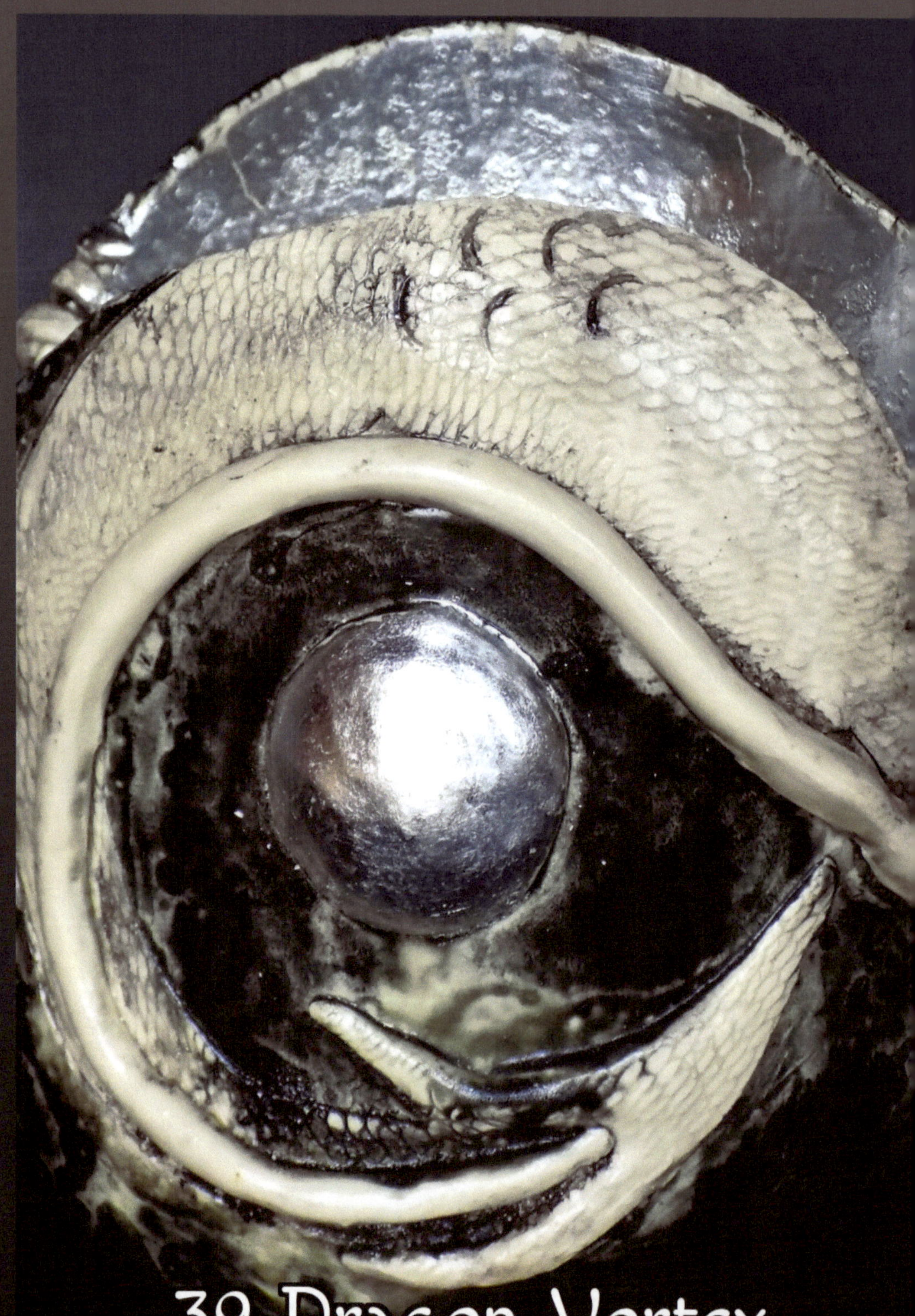
39 Dragon Vortex

Let the dragon energy spin around you.
Feel the power of the vortex.
Manifest your dreams with this powerful
concentration of energy.
What will you manifest?

40 Dragon Energy

Bigger and more potent than anything a human can produce; dragon energy is powerful! Are you prepared to work in such a strong substance as dragon energy?

41 Dragon Story

Dragons love to weave a good story. Let the dragons magnify and embellish your story, until it becomes a great epic adventure for you What is your story?!

42 Dragon Clarity

Our vision is more acute and farther seeing than humans. Let our clarity of sight and of thought work for you.

What seems fuzzy and unclear to you?

43 Dragon Hope

Our hope is always to have the best outcomes in life. What are your hopes? We can assist you in bringing them into existence.

44 Dragon Thought

What we think about appears. Our thoughts become real, almost as soon as we think them. What do you think about? Is it always for your highest and greatest good?

45 Dragon Pearl

We love our treasures. Pearls are precious
forms, created by a small annoyance, that
is transformed into a thing of beauty.
What annoyance do you need
to make into a pearl?

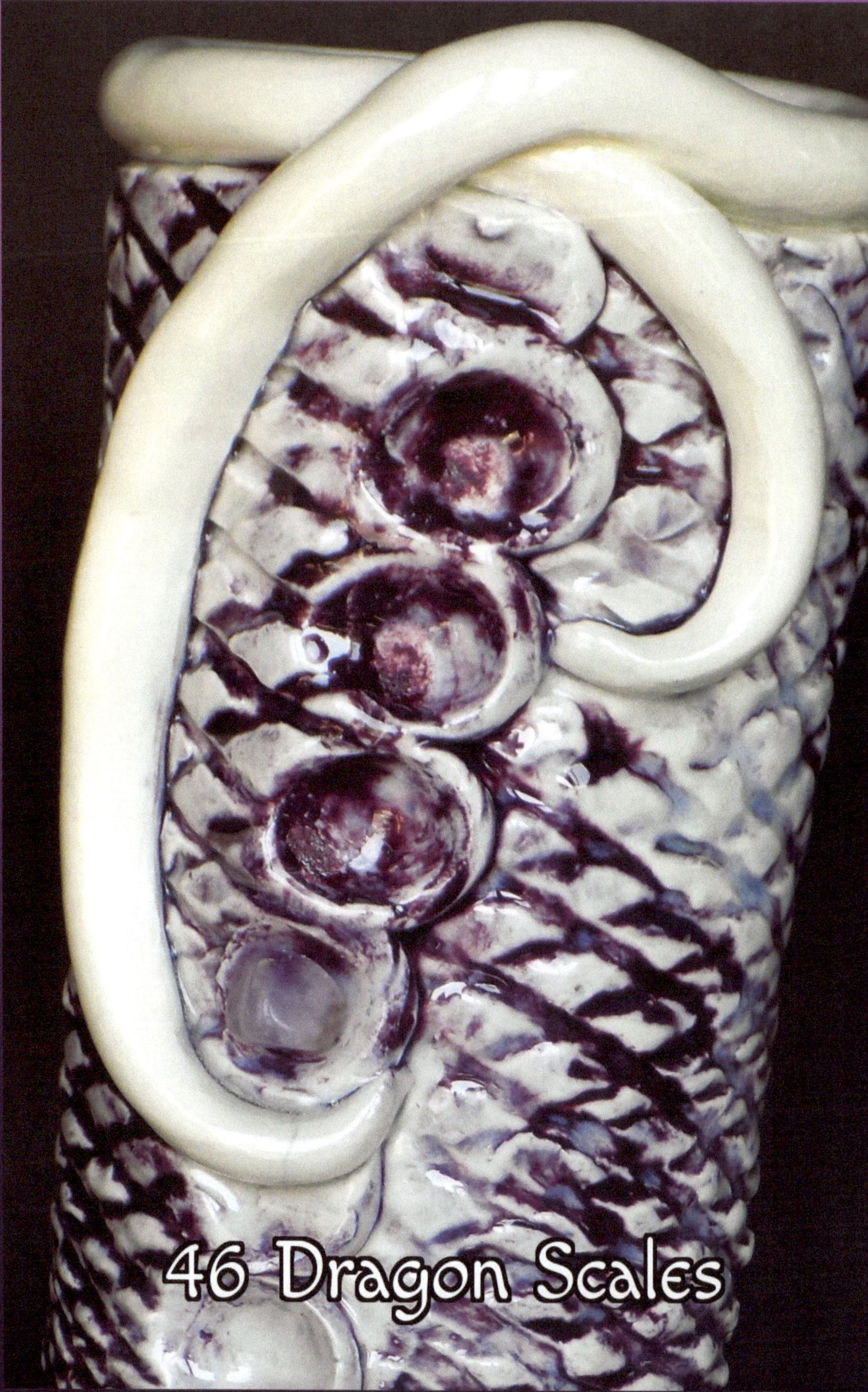

46 Dragon Scales

Our scales are hard and strong. They create our armor. They are part of the reason that we can go through life so unafraid, so bold, so impervious to the things that plague humans. Use our scales as protection when you need it.
How will our scales serve you?

47 Dragon Treasure

Gold, jewels, trinkets large and small, we collect them, we hoard them.
To those that we love, we share our treasures. What treasures do you have?
What treasures do you seek?

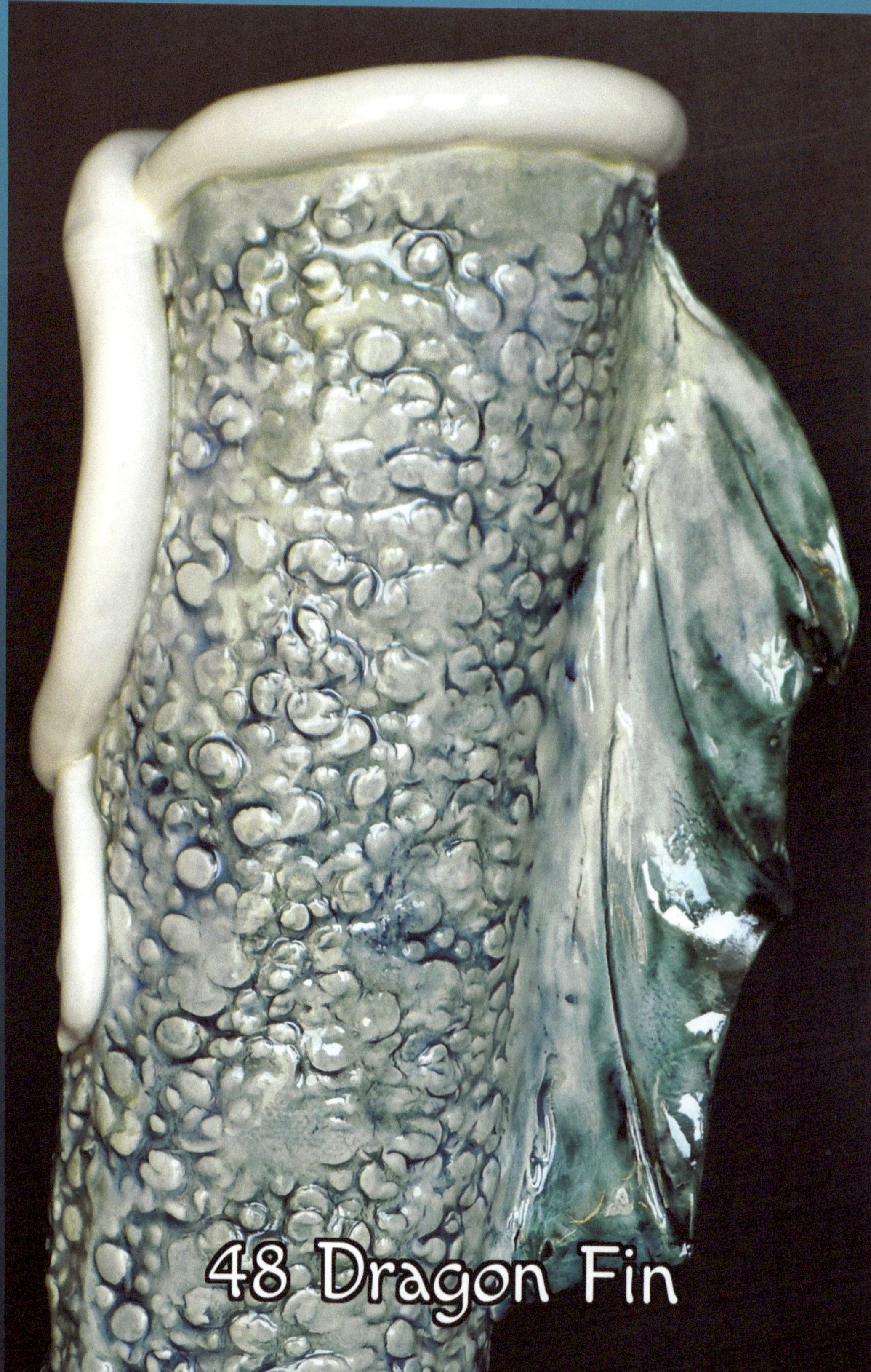

48 Dragon Fin

Water dragons have fanciful fins.
They help with navigation, direction and
the speed of our movement.
What do you need to navigate?
Where do you desire to go?

49 Dragon Wish

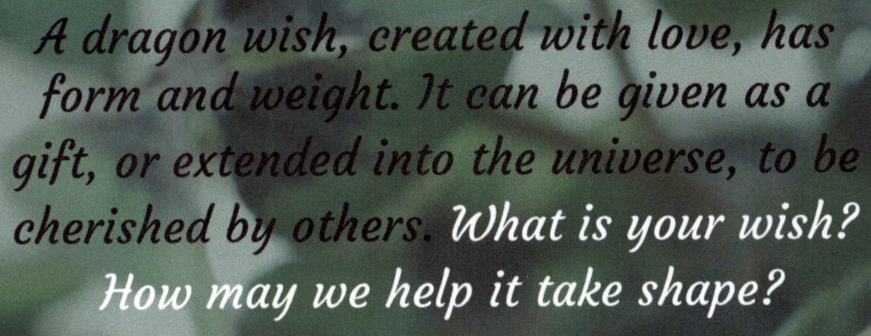

A dragon wish, created with love, has form and weight. It can be given as a gift, or extended into the universe, to be cherished by others. What is your wish? How may we help it take shape?

50 Dragon Longing

Sometimes a thought starts out as a longing.
With time, it will form into an idea, or
tangible thing. What are you longing for?
Is it ready to become a reality?

51 Dragon Direction

Dragons have an unerring sense of direction. We can move through the world without sight, or sound, smell or taste. If we know where we want to go, our bodies will take us there. In what direction are you moving? Is it where you wish to go?

52 The Mud Dragon

"I live in the inner spaces of the planet. I seek the warmth of magma and the boiling beginnings of hot springs. I crave the sulfur and metals from inside the planet's core. Seek me if you need grounding. I will bring you gifts of precious metals and crystals from far underground. *How may I serve you?*"

53 Dragon Eye

Look closer, what do you need to see more clearly? Is there something in your life that needs inspection? Let the dragons guide you in focusing your view.

54 Dragon Spirit

Be one with the dragons. Allow them to
refresh you. Feel the power of
the dragon spirit! Are you now one?

About the Author
Susan Smith James is an artist, potter and author,
living in southern New Jersey with her husband and
two sons. In her first book,
Dancing Dragon Magic: Dialogues in Clay, she used
her dragon pots to illustrate a story about the
dragons who inspired her art. She then took the
photos of her dragon vessels and made Dancing
Dragon Magic Insight Cards, to give others a way to
interact with the dragons. Out of all this, she has
put together a journal, that will move you through
all the dragon personas and subtle energies present
in the book and the cards, to produce a unique
experience for the journaler.
"Enjoy this trip, it is a unique experience for each
traveler, a journey like no other!"
"Everyone should have this much fun!"